It's Time for Bed

Rosey Davidson

Illustrated by
Sophie Kent

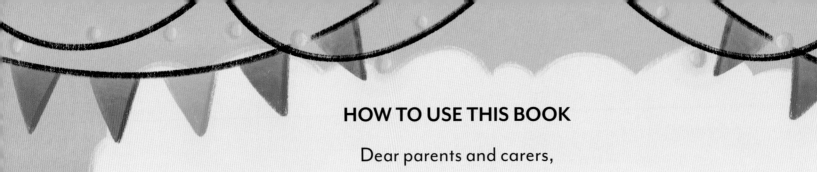

HOW TO USE THIS BOOK

Dear parents and carers,

I really hope this book will help you establish a fun and peaceful bedtime routine. The main story can be read alone to calm and soothe before sleep. The writing in the clouds includes lots of helpful tips that can be just for you, but it can be really useful for children too! So please do also read those parts to your child if it feels appropriate. This book can grow with your child.

Love Rosey

HODDER CHILDREN'S BOOKS
First published in Great Britain in 2024 by
Hodder & Stoughton

13 5 7 9 10 8 6 4 2

PB ISBN 987-1-444-97562-8
E-book ISBN 978-1-444-97940-4

Printed in China

MIX
Paper | Supporting
responsible forestry
FSC® C104740

Hodder Children's Books
An imprint of Hachette Children's Group
Part of Hodder & Stoughton Limited
Carmelite House
50 Victoria Embankment
London, EC4Y 0DZ

An Hachette UK Company
www.hachette.co.uk
www.hachettechildrens.co.uk

It's Time for Bed

Rosey Davidson

Illustrated by
Sophie Kent

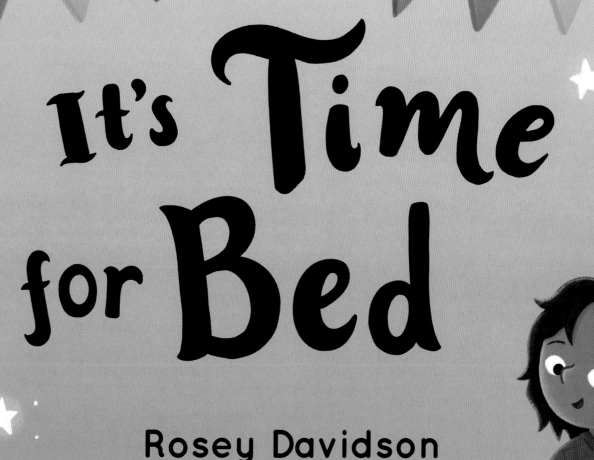

Hodder
Children's
Books

As night-time falls, and the sun goes down, all over the world, grown-ups are saying,

"It's time for bed!"

Having a regular bedtime and wake time can help our bodies know when to feel sleepy. Our bodies have a little clock inside them that likes to know what time we usually do things.

Sometimes we may feel like we want to stay up late, or sleep in, but really our bodies like things to feel the same, or as familiar as possible, each day.

One thing that helps us feel ready for sleep is . . .

bath time!

The warm water in a bath relaxes our muscles, and we get a little cooler when we get out, which helps our bodies know it's time to sleep. Our brains remember what is coming next, which helps us feel safe.

Splish-splashing in the bath keeps us clean and helps us relax as we wash away the day's adventures and get ready for dreamland.

When we get out of the bath,
a hug from our grown-ups
is like being wrapped
up in a warm blanket.

And then it's time to brush our **teeth**
and use the **toilet** or **potty**.

This is very important before bed –
we need to make sure our sweet dreams
aren't interrupted in the night!

We use the potty or toilet
before bed, so that our
tummies can relax for sleep.
Brushing our teeth keeps
the germs away while
we are sleeping.

What are your favourite **pyjamas** like?

Maybe you will choose warm, snuggly pyjamas for chilly nights . . .

16 to 20 degrees Celsius is the room temperature at which our bodies feel the happiest.

. . . Or cool, breezy ones when the weather is warm.

You might have a blanket that feels like a cloud, or a light sheet for hot nights.

If we can't control how hot it is in our room, we can always control our clothing and our bedding. It is important to get air flow into the room, so a window can be opened, if it is safe to do so.

Let's dim the **lights** to make our bedroom lovely and cosy.

That's perfect!

Say goodbye to screens at least an hour before bed. The bright light from these can trick our brains into thinking it's daytime, which makes it harder for us to fall asleep.

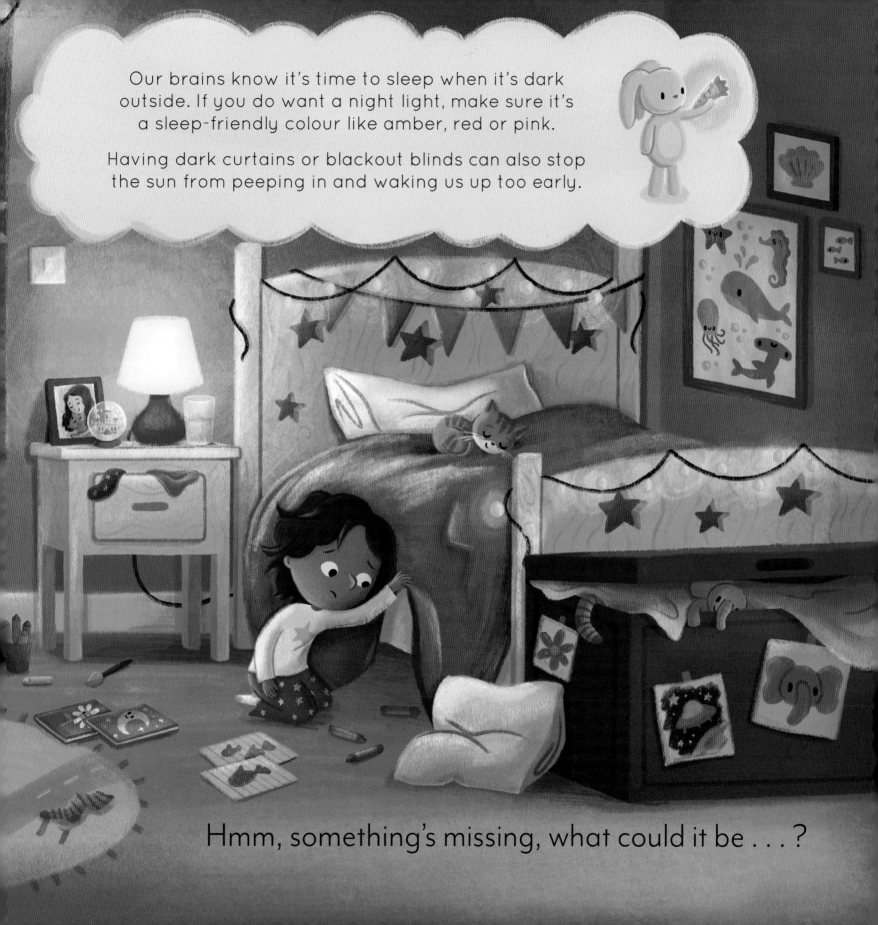

Our brains know it's time to sleep when it's dark outside. If you do want a night light, make sure it's a sleep-friendly colour like amber, red or pink.

Having dark curtains or blackout blinds can also stop the sun from peeping in and waking us up too early.

Hmm, something's missing, what could it be . . . ?

I know – your favourite toy!

Having a special teddy
or blankie with us can
feel like a best friend.
Choosing your favourite
can help you to relax and
sleep well. They can also
help us if we ever sleep
away from home.

Cuddling up with our favourite **blankie** or **teddy** always helps us to feel safe and snug. When we hold onto our teddy or blankie, we are never alone.

We can think about smells that we like, or don't like, at bedtime. You might like your grown-up's perfume, or the smell of your pillow.

Sometimes our brains can feel full of thoughts, and it can be hard to sleep. Try to relax by breathing in through your nose like you are slowly smelling a flower, and breathing out through your mouth like you are blowing out a candle. This will help your body and your mind to get ready for sleep.

Let's pick a **bedtime story!**

A story is a wonderful way to learn about the world, and to spend special time with our grown-ups. Listening to their calm and familiar voice helps us to relax.

Stories can take us to magical worlds, make us **laugh** and **smile**.

Bedtime is the perfect time for a story!

Let's **snuggle up**, so our grown-ups can read us our bedtime story.

Sharing a story together can make us feel happier about our bedtime routine and going to bed.

Before we close our eyes at night, it can be helpful to think of something that made us happy during the day, and something that we are excited about.

Safe in our grown-up's arms,
sleep isn't far away.

And as our eyes grow heavy,
we **cuddle** closer.

As you grow, you will learn to fall asleep on your own. Remember, your bed is the safest place you can be, with your grown-ups always close by.

Gentle relaxation can really help us – some deep breathing, quiet reading or connecting with our grown-ups through talking.

Our bedtime **kiss** and cuddle can help us

let go of our daytime worries.

When the light is turned off,
we feel safe and snug in our bed.

Sometimes we might need to use the
toilet, have a drink of water or take off
a layer of clothing. But sometimes we
don't wake at all until the morning!

As you drift off to **sleep**, other children all around the world are doing the same.

There is no right or wrong when it comes to sleep, it's about what works for you and your family.

Good night, everyone!
Sleep tight.

Everyone needs to sleep
well to feel happy and
healthy. What is important
is that we aren't afraid to
do things differently if they
aren't working. Babies,
children and grown-ups
all need their rest.

Activities to Try With Your Child

Let out the angry bees

Sit or lay down and listen to your breath going in and out.

Take a deep breath.

Squeeze your fists into balls and imagine that they are heating up with all the things that have made you feel cross today.

Your thoughts are buzzing like angry bees!

Keep breathing, in and out.

Take a big breath in, and as you breathe out open your hands and let go of all your worries as they fly off into the night sky.

Find your safe place

Lay down on the floor, or in your bed. Close your eyes. Take a deep breath and think about a happy place – somewhere you feel safe.

Imagine yourself exploring that place – what can you hear? Can you hear water, or a bird? Can you smell flowers, or the salty sea? What can you touch there? A tree, a rock, or sand? Perhaps you have you found something special there.

Say goodbye to your special place and return back to your bed.

Open your eyes gently and remember where you are. Think about your special place whenever you feel worried. Remember that you are safe in your bed.

Set up a sleep-friendly bedroom

Create a calming bedroom that is clear of clutter.

It's better for bedrooms to be slightly on the cooler side for sleep (16 to 18 degrees Celsius is ideal).

Choose cotton, breathable bedding and sleepwear – be mindful of your child's own preferences, for example if labels annoy them, or strong-smelling washing powder disturbs them.

Blackout blinds are very helpful, especially with little ones who tend to wake early, or struggle to settle when it's still light outside or if streetlights are close by.

Some children may sleep better with a night light but be sure to choose a sleep-friendly colour, such as amber, orange, red or pink. These colours don't interfere with the process of us falling asleep, whereas white lights tell us it's time to wake up and can affect our melatonin production (one of our sleep hormones).

Include a favourite teddy, or comforter if your child likes it.

Keep a drink of water nearby.

Tech and screen time

Try to switch off devices at least an hour before bed. This will help your child to unwind and allow the body and mind to relax.

Focus on quieter activities, or connection time with you. Bedtime stories are a great way to help your child to unwind and have a positive effect on their mental wellbeing. They are an opportunity to learn, but also to relax and spend time with you.

Reading a book with your child is a great learning opportunity for them, but it also provides a way for you to be physically close to each other too. It is very calming as part of their bedtime wind-down.

The bedtime routine

A predictable routine, similar every evening. The same things in the same order. Try to keep their bedtime (and their wake time in the morning!), roughly the same each day. This helps their internal body clocks.

The timing needs to be right – not too early, and not too late. If it's too late, children may become upset or hard to calm. If it's too early, it may take children a long time to get to sleep, and this can cause bedtime battles.

Try not to rush – children can sense if you rush. They want to enjoy the connection time with you before you are separated for the night.

You can create loving boundaries. Children like to know what is coming next, and that you stick to what you have said. They might try to test those boundaries, which is very normal, but it's important for you to stick to what you have agreed.

Give children some autonomy, for example, allowing them to choose their pyjamas and stories.

Quiet reflection

Think about someone you love – maybe it's a friend or your grown-up.

Think about when you last saw them, or something you did together, or something they said that made you feel safe and happy.

Write it down on a piece of paper, if you can, or create a drawing about it.

Stick it up next to your bed.

Roll like a ball, rock like a star

Sit on the floor and close your eyes.

Start slowly rocking your body from side to side. Breathe in and out as you rock in time with your breathing.

See how slowly you can rock.

Next, lay on your back and curl up into a ball. Hold your knees into your chest.

Rock to one side and then the other, keeping in time with your breath.

Roll forward and backwards too.

When you're ready to stop, stay still for a moment and take three deep breaths in and out.

This book is for all the little dreamers out there.
May you love your bed and sleep, always.
And for my own babies, thank you for giving me the
joy of reading you a bedtime story ~ *R.D.*

This book is dedicated to Josh – thanks for
always believing in me ~ *S.K.*